This book belongs to:

....

Based on the episode "Paddington and the Love Day Cards" by Hannah George

Adapted by Lauren Holowaty

First published in Great Britain by
HarperCollins *Children's Books* in 2021
HarperCollins *Children's Books* is a division of HarperCollins*Publishers* Ltd,
HarperCollins Publishers
1 London Bridge Street
London SE1 9GF

The HarperCollins website address is:
www.harpercollins.co.uk

1 3 5 7 9 10 8 6 4 2

ISBN: 978-0-00-840917-3

Printed in Italy

Based on the Paddington novels written and created by Michael Bond

MIX
Paper from
responsible sources
FSC® C007454

FSC is a non-profit international organisation established to promote the
responsible management of the world's forests. Products carrying the FSC
label are independently certified to assure consumers that they come
from forests that are managed to meet the social, economic and
ecological needs of present and future generations.

Find out more about HarperCollins and the environment at
www.harpercollins.co.uk/green

The Adventures of Paddington™

Love Day

HarperCollins *Children's Books*

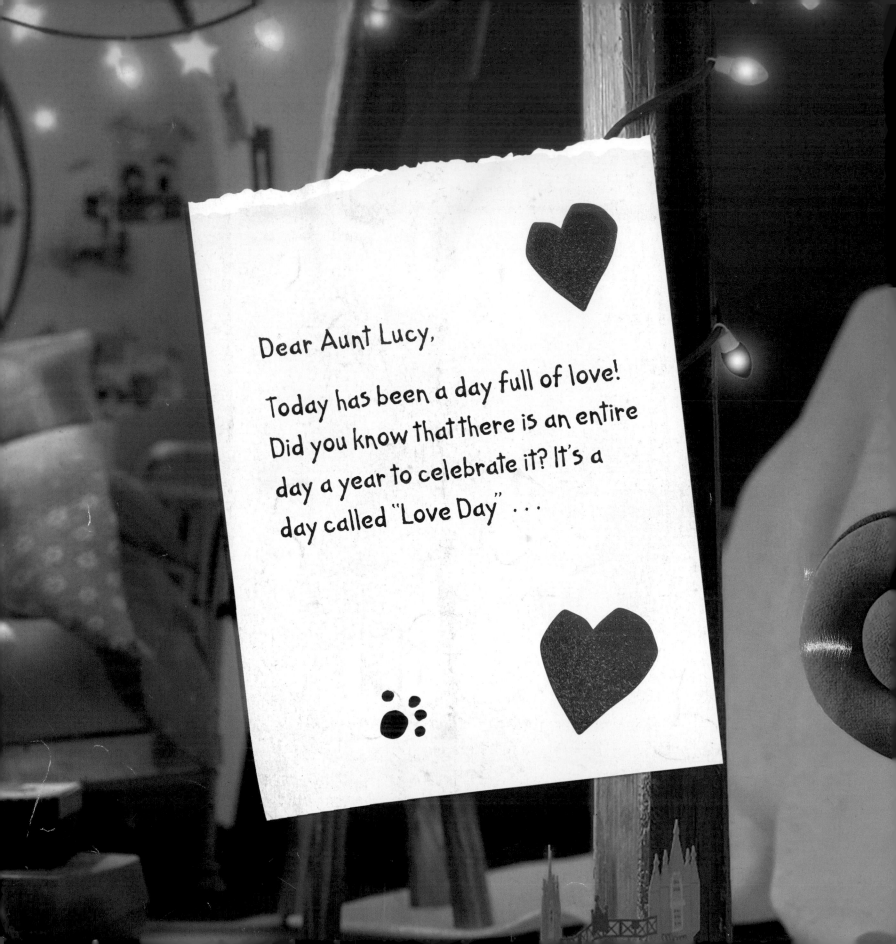

Dear Aunt Lucy,

Today has been a day full of love!
Did you know that there is an entire
day a year to celebrate it? It's a
day called "Love Day" . . .

"Happy Love Day!"

said Mr Brown, surprising
Mrs Brown with a special heart-
shaped breakfast.

"What's Love Day?"

asked Paddington, popping up
at the table. "It sounds like a jolly
nice day."

"It is," replied Mrs Brown.
"It's about letting the people you
love know that you love them."

"Happy Love Day, everyone!" said Mrs Bird as she walked in, carrying a large bag of Love Day cards.

Mrs Brown reminded her about **the special treat** they had in store that evening. "Mr Brown is taking us all to the Columbian café in the park to celebrate. He booked it *weeks* ago . . ."

"EEEEAAAAH!"

Mr Brown dropped the saucepan into the sink with a **SPLASH!**

"You **haven't forgotten** to book the café, have you, darling?" asked Mrs Brown, looking worried.

"**Nooo-hoo-hoo.** Of course not," spluttered Mr Brown, rushing out.

But Mr Brown *had* forgotten! He hurried to the park
with Judy and Jonathan to see if he could book a table for that
evening. On the way, they bumped into Mateo and his dog,
Lucky, whose lead got wrapped round Mr Brown's scooter.

When Lucky spotted a squirrel,
he went charging after it,
dragging Mr Brown with him!

"NOOOOOO, LUCKY! SSSTOP!"

After pulling Mr Brown around the whole park, Lucky finally **skidded to a halt** outside the Columbian café. He sat proudly in front of Jonathan, Judy and Mateo while Mr Brown tried to recover.

Woof!

Once he'd got his breath back, Mr Brown begged Sofia for a table for the Love Day dinner. But she said the café was fully booked!

"Nooooo!" cried Mr Brown.

Then Sofia had an idea. "If we push some tables together, I can squeeze you in."

"Oh, thank you, thank you!" said a relieved Mr Brown.

Meanwhile, Paddington had made a special Love Day
card for Mrs Bird.

"Thank you, Paddington," she replied, admiring his
handiwork. "That's very kind of you."

But Paddington hadn't just made one Love Day card – he'd made a **whole stack** of them. "Mrs Bird, could you help me deliver these, please?"

"Goodness, Paddington!" gasped Mrs Bird. "You have made a lot of friends since arriving from Peru."

"Yes, I suppose I have," agreed Paddington. "I've made cards for *everyone*."

Mrs Bird took Paddington out on her motorcycle to deliver his Love Day cards.

BURROOOM BOOM, BOOM!

"Happy Love Day, Pigeonton!" Paddington called to his feathered friend. "I've made you a caaarrr—"

WHOOSH!

A great gust of wind blew Paddington's cards clean out of his paws . . .

"Oh bother!" cried Paddington as his cards were scattered far and wide. "Don't worry," said Mrs Bird, dropping Paddington off on the pavement. "I'll get them back." And with that she zoomed away!

As Paddington walked along the road, the wind whipped another of his cards past him and into Mr Gruber's antiques shop. Inside, Paddington spotted the card stuck in a suit of armour.

"There you are!"

WAAAAH!

Paddington couldn't reach it so he climbed on to a globe, but it began to **spin round and round!** He'd just managed to grab the card when the suit of armour toppled towards him with a . . .

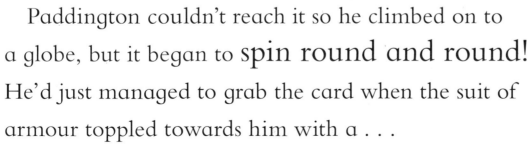

CERRRAASHHH!

"Goodness me, Paddington!" said Mr Gruber, hearing the kerfuffle. "What's going on?" He looked down to see his suit of armour in pieces on the floor and Paddington wearing the helmet!

"Happy Love Day, Mr Gruber!" called Paddington. Just then, the helmet fell over his eyes . . .

CLANG!

"Thank you, Paddington," chuckled Mr Gruber. "Happy Love Day to you too."

After leaving Mr Gruber's shop, Paddington noticed
Pigeonton had found one of his Love Day cards caught on
the bunting outside.

"Well done, Pigeonton!" he called as he climbed
up to get it . . .

Paddington walked carefully along the bunting, but when he reached

the middle it got very wobbly . . .

"WHHOOOAAA!" BOING!

The poor bear was flipped up into the air and left hanging

from one foot – upside down!

"I appear to be rather tied up," he said with a sigh.

Mrs Bird spotted Paddington dangling from the bunting. "How on earth did *you* get up there, wee cub?" she said, climbing up to get him. "Now let's get you free. We've only one more card to find."

But just as Mrs Bird untangled Paddington the bunting snapped and they both swung down towards the ground . . .

"WHOOOAAA!"

PLOP!

Mrs Bird landed perfectly
on her motorbike and . . .

CRASH!

Paddington landed in the rubbish bin!

"I found the last card!" cheered Paddington, spotting it in the bottom of the bin.

"Clever wee cub!" said Mrs Bird. "Jump on and we'll go straight to the park!" And off they sped!

Mrs Bird and Paddington reached the café just as it was turning to dusk. The Browns were waiting for them.

"Hello, everyone," began Paddington. "I've got cards for you all – Aaahhhh!"

Paddington tripped and his cards went flying . . .

. . . landing on the grass just as the park keeper was mowing the lawn.

CRRRUNNNCH!

The park keeper accidentally cut them into hundreds of pieces with his lawnmower!

"Oh no!" gasped Paddington. "My Love Day cards!"

"Now no one will know that I love them on Love Day," said Paddington sadly.

"Cards aren't the *only* way to show people you love them," Mrs Brown said. "You show us every day by being such a lovely bear."